Never Make A Promise

Fatima Munroe

TEXT UCP TO 22828 TO SUBSCRIBE TO OUR MAILING LIST

If you would like to join our team, submit the first 3-4 chapters of your completed manuscript to

Submissions@UrbanChapterspublications.com

A Note From Fatima

Have you read *Thick Thighs Save Lives Volume 1*? Keyon and Leonie are from the short story *Stay* that I contributed to this anthology. The plan was to write the story for the anthology and finish a few other projects I had going on, but I've received a lot of inboxes asking if I would be releasing the full novel. For Valentine's Day, I decided to expand on their story. This book is what I considered to be the deleted scenes, lol! If you've read it, I've added a few sentences here, a paragraph there, reworked a few of the chapters, and changed the ending. If you haven't read it, it's a love story between a man and a woman that'll renew your faith in love at first sight. Either way, I hope you enjoy it!

Fatima Munroe

Chapter 1

Three years ago

"I'll have the apple walnut salad and a cold glass of water with a slice of lemon," I said to the waitress without looking at the menu.

"That's all you want?" Tristan barked as his eyes grazed the menu. "Since she ain't eating, gimme the buttermilk fried chicken breast with the cracked pepper biscuit, collard greens, make those mashed potatoes with garlic and extra butter, and substitute the creamed corn for the jasmine rice pirloo," he finished as he passed the waitress the menu.

"Anything to drink, sir?"

"Yea, gimme the uh…" He snatched the menu from the waitress' hand and perused the wine selection. "Gimme a bottle of the Hamilton Russell Walker Bay Chardonnay. Thanks."

The waitress nodded her head as she furiously scribbled his request on her order pad. "Thank you, sir. I'll get this put in as soon as possible."

Tristan turned his back to her and focused on me. "Our six month anniversary. I bring you to Magnolia's, the most exclusive restaurant in Charleston, and the best you can do is a fruit salad and a glass of lemon water?"

"Honey, I'm not hungry." I tried being nice to soothe the irritated scowl on his face.

"You ain't hungry?" he chided dismally. "I find that hard to believe. Stop lying to yourself and get you a steak to go with that salad!"

I turned my face in embarrassment; Tristan had gone too far this time. In the six months we'd been together, he reserved his insults for when we were behind closed doors. This was the first time we were in mixed company and he joked about my weight. Even the couple at the table beside ours appeared uncomfortable.

"Tristan, please. Not here, and not now," I spoke in a muted tone.

"Why not? We're in a restaurant, right? Isn't this your second home?" he sneered, laughing wildly.

"I'm not going to do this with you tonight." I stood up and threw my napkin on the table just as the waitress brought out our meals. "Call me when you get it together."

Leaving him sitting with a childish smirk on his face, I grabbed my purse and walked out of the restaurant. A few of the restaurant patrons gave me smiles and thumbs up gestures as I left with my head held high. What they didn't know was that when Tristan showed up on my doorstep to apologize in thirty minutes, I would accept it with open arms.

∞

Tristan and I met six months ago at the gym; he was getting out of the pool, and I was debating on getting in. His charismatic good looks had held me hostage ever since I joined the gym three weeks prior, and I was in shock that he encouraged me to face my fears. I had always been the 'big' girl; ever since I had a growth spurt in the fifth grade, I'd been called all sorts of names. Kids can be cruel, but it was what their parents whispered about me when they thought I wasn't listening that affected my self-esteem the most. My best friend suddenly wasn't allowed to play with me anymore because her mother thought I was 'fast', messing around with boys and letting them touch my body.

According to her, that's why my breasts were so big and my hips spread so quickly. Growing up in the south, I was the victim of so many old wives' tales that had nothing to do with me, but alienated me from having a social life.

I turned to food as a comforter, friend, and confidant. German chocolate cake was my listening ear, Lay's potato chips were my best girlfriend that told me we should hang out more often, and a two liter of Pepsi explained to me every other day that I would be fine. By the time I hit high school, I was almost one hundred pounds overweight, and teased constantly. The first time I had sex wasn't a memorable moment for me; it was done on a dare. At the time, I didn't know that the words whispered to me in the heat of passion by the captain of the football team were a lie until the videotape surfaced, and by then, it was all over the school. Dropping out after that incident, I went and got my GED, then enrolled in college at the age of seventeen. Walking across the stage to receive my master's degree from the Medical University of South Carolina on my twenty-third birthday was my personal gift to myself.

Settling into a career as a lab manager, my days weren't exactly full of running around an office to make sure deadlines were completed and disciplining employees.

On the contrary, I sat at my desk and shuffled paperwork while sending and reading emails all day long. I had traded in listening to food for advice to actual living and breathing people, and one of the doctors, Nyoka, who was a good friend of mine, sat me down for a heart to heart. She gave it to me straight, informing me that I was morbidly obese and would be a great candidate for bariatric surgery. I declined; the thought of someone cutting on my body wasn't appealing at all. She then recommended a gym near the hospital so I wouldn't have to be faced with the embarrassment from my peers seeing me in gym clothes, and we signed up for classes together. I didn't think she needed it; she was smaller than me, but I agreed. So, every other day, we were working out and getting fit.

After changing my diet and eating healthy, combined with strength training, I began to see results. Yes, the women at Gold's Gym would point at me and laugh when I did jumping jacks or jumped rope, but surprisingly, the men would give me approving nods and encouraging words. A few of the bodybuilder types would ask me out from time to time, but I could tell by the look in their eyes what they wanted. Tristan was the only one who took the time to get to know me first.

We went from workout partners to friends to dating. In the beginning, everything was perfect. Tristan would compliment me on my hair, my clothes, my perfume. He even invited me to meet his parents. I just knew then that he looked at our relationship as something more than just a fling; he could see himself with me for the long haul. I'd never been more wrong about anything in my entire life. His father was charming, but his mother was a piece of work. Purposely loading my plate up with fattening foods, offering me more bread, more butter, more saturated fat, in my opinion. Making slick comments about my size under her breath. If I wasn't a southern belle, I would've cussed her miserable ass out.

After that disastrous night, Tristan's attitude toward me changed; gone was the kindhearted man that I fell in love with, replaced by the crude and insensitive minion that his mother created. I knew I should've ran away from him yelling and screaming, but my heart wouldn't allow me to leave. Tristan would sometimes insult me to the point of tears, then apologize for his behavior, begging for my forgiveness. I wanted him so much that I took him back every time, knowing deep down that he was wrong. I just couldn't let him go.

Chapter 2

"Leonie! Baby, you know I didn't mean it! Open the door, let's talk about this, ok? I love you," Tristan's voice called to me through the door.

Standing with my back against the door, I allowed the tears to flow freely down my face. He was saying all the right things, and I wanted to fling the door open to take advantage of this night; our anniversary night. But, that voice in the back of my head that normally whispers to me that I needed to move on was now screaming loudly in hi-definition, clear as day.

"No, Tristan! Why would you say those cruel things to me? If you truly loved me, we wouldn't be going through this!"

"Open this damn door, Leonie! I'm not playing; if you don't open this door, I'm leaving! You want me to leave? HUH!"

Let him go, the voice in my head begged as I unlocked the locks, turning the knob and snatching the door open. Tristan walked into my open arms and rested his head on my cleavage.

"I'm sorry I left you sitting in the restaurant, Tris. But, you hurt me," I spoke my truth as silent tears dropped from my orbs.

"I didn't mean to hurt you, Leonie. Sometimes, I just can't help myself," he mumbled, his mouth full of the material covering my breasts. Using his teeth, he moved my shirt to the side and nibbled at my nipples through the thin lace barely covering me from being completely naked. "Do you forgive me, love?"

"Yes," I breathed, my eyelids fluttering while his hand moved downward and I felt the breeze from outside on my upper thighs. Tristan raised my dress and was trying to pull down my panties as he used his other hand to unhook my bra. "Lemme... lemme close the door first."

He kicked the door closed while sucking hickeys on my chest, not missing a beat.

"Leonie, baby lemme make it up to you, ok?" he mumbled as he walked forward, clutching me tightly, causing me to walk backward into the living room. Gently guiding me toward the couch, he leaned me back and laid me across the couch with his hand furiously kneading my clit until it was fully engorged. I whimpered for him to stop while guiding his head downward to meet my hidden treasure. He got the hint, kissing down my body until he reached my panties, licking my sweetness through the black lace.

"Is this what you want me to do, girl? You want me to taste your pussy?"

I nodded, anticipating the soft touch from his mouth that never came. Instead, I was met with his member smacking me in the face. "Feel like playing the flute tonight?"

"Flute? I thought you were making it up to me." I opened my eyes, confused. This was MY night; I was the one embarrassed. And to make it up to HIM, I had to put MY mouth on HIM?

"I am, baby. I am. But, I can't get in the mood unless you give me a little mouth first, you know that. Come on, baby," he coaxed with his penis closer to my lips. "You left me in the restaurant by myself, I had to pay for all that food. I'm not mad about that, though. Do this for me, ok?"

Begrudgingly, I opened my mouth and wrapped my lips around his member. He closed his eyes as I deep throated his cock, moaning as he thrust himself in and out of my mouth. I felt his pace quicken, and the vein underneath was firm against my tongue. I hurried up and moved my mouth when I tasted the first salty drop on my tonsils, pissed that he was coming and I wasn't.

"AHHH!" his screams echoed throughout the foyer. "SHIT! That was good, baby," he spoke as he spilled his seed onto my marbled floor tile before tucking his member back into his underwear and zipping his pants up. "That was real good. You gonna be aight, right?"

"Are you leaving?"

"Well, you know I gotta work in the morning," he spoke as he searched for his keys. "Damn, I forgot I didn't drive, Uber dropped me off. Where your keys?"

"Tristan, I have to work in the morning too," I sulked as I pulled my dress down and adjusted my shirt. "Call your roommate and have him come and pick you up."

"My roommate ain't coming all the way out here this time of night! Come on now, Leonie, I'll bring your car back tomorrow, damn! You can take a cab to work," he grumbled.

"No, Tristan." I was firm; this time I wasn't falling for his mess.

"You must be scared that your man gonna catch me in your car, huh," he started up with his usual bullshit. "That's why I can't drive your car, ain't it?"

My phone rang just as I was about to answer him. Snatching my purse from the couch, Tristan dug through my personal things until he found it and stared pointedly at the screen.

"It's your mother," his curiosity satiated, he threw my phone at me. I caught it in midair and answered the call, turning my back to him.

"Hello, Mama?" Listening to her conversation, I temporarily forgot that Tristan and I were in the middle of a disagreement until I glanced out the living room window and saw headlights rapidly disappearing down my driveway. "Mama, let me call you back, ok?" Waiting until she hung up, I then dialed 911 to report my car stolen. Tristan had finally tap danced on my last nerve.

∞

"So, this Tristan person is your boyfriend, right?" Officer Keyon asked as he took the report. "What's his last name again?"

I nodded my head in agreement, until he asked me that question. In the six months since I'd known him, I never knew his last name. *I never knew his last name. What is wrong with me? Giving my body to a man that I knew nothing about?*

"I'm—I'm not sure what his last name is," I dropped my voice so that the officer didn't lecture me on how stupid I was.

"You know, this happens a lot more than you might think it does." He stopped taking the report to inform me about the men who purposely prey on women. "Someone like you could be perceived as weak, a perfect mark for these type of men."

"Someone like me? What's that supposed to mean?" I gave him an angry stare, hands planted firmly on my hips. If I had to, I would sit in jail for slapping the taste out of his mouth.

"I don't mean any harm," he retreated quickly from his words to me a moment ago. "What I'm saying is that a beautiful woman such as yourself could easily be mistaken for weak. Judging from your response, I know for a fact that's not you."

My face suddenly felt hot, and I turned away from his friendly smile. "So, uhm, do you think you'll be able to find my car, Officer—"

"Call me Keyon," he spoke warmly. "And yes, I know I can find your car. Don't worry about anything. Just try to get some rest, ok Leonie? You're safe, trust me."

"Trust you?" I croaked somberly. "Last man I trusted stole my car."

"Yea, trust me. Kids steal cars; you talking to a grown man now," Keyon chuckled smugly, tucking his notepad into his shirt pocket. "I'll call you in the morning, ok?"

"Ok," I couldn't help but to blush for a second time. Keyon made me feel something I'd never felt before, and I didn't know what to think.

Chapter 3

"Leonie, call the station and tell them it was just a misunderstanding! Tell them you want to drop the charges!" Tristan's tone was urgent on my voicemail. True to his word, Keyon found my car last night, parked in front of a single-family home on the edge of a subdivision in North Charleston. I dropped him off at an apartment complex downtown a few times, where I knew he lived with his roommate. Or did he? Who the hell lived in North Charleston?

Deleting his messages, I turned my attention back to the email currently on my screen. Nyoka sent me a message about our personal training class being cancelled that evening, and she wanted to know if I was willing to go out for drinks; I politely declined. Keyon sent me a text a few minutes prior asking if he could stop by to drop off my car and give me an update on my case. His tone was urgent, so I wanted to make sure he had my full attention.

For the first time since I took the job, my team was finished with their work early and I let everyone go home, saving myself a couple of dollars in payroll. Cruising over the bridge to my home across the water in Mount Pleasant, I turned up the radio in my rental and sang along with Trey

Songz as he crooned a song that was the soundtrack to my life at that moment:

In too deep, can't think about giving it up

But I never knew love would feel like a heart attack

It's killing me, swear I never cried so much

Cause I never knew love would hurt this fucking bad

Worst pain that I ever had

Even though it was less than twenty-four hours, I was starting to see Tristan in a different light, the light I should've saw him in all along. He didn't want me; he wanted what he felt like I could do for him. Give him money, cater to him, and give him sex on demand. He wanted marriage perks without the title. Tristan saw me as his submissive wife that he had no plans on walking down the aisle. It hurt like hell when the truth showed up and punched you in the face, especially when you realized that you were defeated in the first round of this thing called a 'relationship'.

The crazy thing is that I thought Tristan loved me. I really thought he loved me. Through the name calling, the body shaming, the forced sexual acts that I performed for his acceptance, I really thought in some sick, twisted way that Tristan loved me; he just had a unique way of showing it. It was time for me to get my shit together and love myself. I had to love ME before anyone else could. I needed to be happy with myself, by myself. How could I give love if I never really knew what it was? My first love was a joke, and it looked like my second love was too.

Pulling up to my townhouse, I saw the cruiser sitting at the curb and smiled inside; the highlight of my day would be seeing Officer Keyon again. Parking my car in my driveway, I watched him get out of the police cruiser and saunter toward my vehicle.

"Just got off work?" He flashed a set of pearly white teeth with pink gums and no spaces in my direction.

"Yea. Been waiting long?"

"I just got here a few minutes ago."

"Oh ok. Well, come on in then," I invited him inside.

He followed me, holding the door open once I got the key turned in the lock. Stepping in behind me, he even took off his shoes at the door before accepting my invitation to take a seat on the couch.

"So Leonie, first things first. Got something that you've been worried about," he spoke, digging into his pocket and pulling out the keys to my BMW. "A few scratches on the leather, but other than that, your car is in pretty good condition. Second, I wanted to discuss with you what we found out about your boyfriend, Tristan."

"What about him?"

"Well," Keyon began, grabbing the folder that was tucked under his arm, "His real name isn't Tristan. It's James."

"James? James who?" I asked with a raised eyebrow.

"James Montgomery. It appears that Mr. Montgomery is what we at the precinct like to call a hobosapien," he snickered.

"A hobosapien? What's that? Do I need to go get checked out?"

"No, no, no, nothing like that. Mr. Montgomery is one of those men that will start a relationship with a woman, strictly to have a roof over his head."

"What?"

"He hangs around the gym and preys on women. Usually, he'll make friends with a woman sometime around the beginning of the year, when everyone floods the gym to start working on those New Year's   resolutions. Once he selects his bait, he goes in for the kill; complimenting their efforts, giving tips to enhance training, exchanging phone numbers for 'personal training', and it just goes from there. Does any of that sound familiar?"

I sat stone faced for a second before I busted out laughing. "You mean to tell me that the man I was calling my man ain't nothing but a bum out here tricking women?" Keyon nodded his head up and down, staring at me strangely. "Wait, he had a roommate. I dropped him off more than once!" I screamed hysterically.

"About that. The address that you gave us is actually his mother's address."

"HIS MOTHER!" I roared, pissed to the max by this point. "Wait, his mother doesn't live in an apartment. She lives in a house on Sullivan's Island."

"No, his aunt lives in a house on Sullivan's Island with her wealthy husband. His aunt who won't allow him to come and live with her but does put her stamp of approval on anyone he dates."

"Ain't this boutta bitch!" I fumed. "I should've cussed that old bitch out when I had the chance!"

"So, do you want to drop the charges, or—"

"Hell naw, I ain't dropping the charges! Where did you get that from?"

"Well, Mr. Montgomery seems to be under the impression that you're on your way to the station to explain that this was all just a miscommunication between you two. I asked him how Mrs. Montgomery would feel about —"

"MRS. MONTGOMERY! WHO THE FUCK IS SHE?"

"Mr. Montgomery's common-law wife," Keyon smirked, but I didn't find a damn thing funny.

"Keyon, you lying!" He handed me the folder to read for myself, and it was all right there in black and white.

"Leonie, I hate to be the bearer of bad news, but this is something that I felt like you should know."

The ink started to run, and I realized it was from the wetness pouring from my eyes. "I—I can't believe I was so STUPID!"

"I don't think you were stupid, Leonie. A beautiful, vivacious woman like you was just looking for her Boaz. You just ran into Pookie instead, that's all," he spoke gently as he moved closer to me and patted my hand.

"What is wrong with me, Keyon? I'm human, dammit! I just want to be loved, just like anyone else out here! Aren't I worth that?" I sobbed on his shoulder as he ran his fingers through my hair and rubbed my back.

"You're worth that, plus more, baby," his voice murmured in my ear. "You're worth so much more. You just gotta know your worth and stop giving yourself away for the sake of saying you got somebody."

I nodded at his words; Keyon was right. It felt good to hear someone verbalize what was going on in my head at that exact moment. "I'm sorry, I messed up your uniform," I began, embarrassed that a total stranger caught me in a vulnerable moment.

"Uhm— don't, don't worry about it," he fumbled over his words, and I saw his expression change. "I don't live too far from here, I'll run home and grab another one."

"Uhm, thank you for the information." I was genuinely appreciative of his extra effort; he didn't have to dig into Tristan's— I meant James' background like that.

"Anytime, Leoni. I go the extra mile for those that I— well, I hate to see a damsel in distress. Give me a call if you're in a bind again, ok?"

"Ok," I smiled as I walked him to the door. Watching him walk to his car, I wondered what he left unsaid. Was Keyon trying to imply that he wanted to— nah. I was reading too much into someone just doing their job and being nice.

Finally closing and locking the door once the cruiser pulled off, I walked over and sat down on the chaise lounge chair in my living room to think over my life. It was officially over between Tristan and I. This latest stunt of his was the nail in the coffin where I buried my relationship. In full mourning mode, I openly bawled at my misfortune; the time out of my life that I spent in a dead-end affair with a man who was incapable of love. I take that back, a man who was incapable of loving ME. Tristan was incapable of loving ME. I wanted so badly to be with him, so badly to be with someone who reciprocated my feelings. I couldn't understand what was wrong with me, why the women around me all had successful relationships; living forever in happily matrimonial bliss while I was the miserable one still searching for someone to complete me. Did I not deserve to be loved too?

Hearing what I thought was a noise in the kitchen, I stood up and headed to where the sound came from. Passing an ornate, neoclassical mirror in my living room, I stopped when I caught a glimpse of the reflection staring back at me: unloved, devoid of life, ready to give up on the world and herself. At that very moment, I realized what my mama had been trying to tell me all those years growing up as the 'big' girl: it didn't matter what people thought of me as long as I loved the person staring back at me in that mirror.

Did I love that reflection? Was the broken down woman staring back at me in the mirror worth love, capable of loving someone else? I stared directly into her pupils and examined her soul through the red rimmed lids staring back at me. Raising my hand to touch her lips, I caressed her face as the wetness halted on my cheeks; tasted the saltiness of the wisps of tears that served as a monument of how SHE was exploited for the one thing that should've been held near and dear to her: her heart. Her identity. Her capacity to love and share that feeling with another person. I forgot about HER.

"I'm sorry, Leonie," I whispered to that reflection, that woman whose heart lay shattered in a thousand pieces lying exposed for the world to see, to be the subject of ridicule. "I should have loved you. Make no mistake, love, WE will never be in this position again," I spoke with a newfound resolve. The beauty in the mirror wiped her face with the back of her hand before I leaned forward and planted those same lips against the glass, forever infatuated with myself from that moment forward.

Chapter 4

Tristan, James— whoever he was calling himself lately— had been calling me for a few weeks, and each time I saw the number for the corrections department show up on my phone, I ignored it. Keyon arrested him at his house in front of his common-law wife, and I knew she was just as shocked as I was to find out that he was living a double life. I know if it was me and I found out that a man I called myself in love with wasn't who I thought he was, I'd want some answers.

In the meantime, life at the lab was crazy as ever. We got a huge order from a facility in Atlanta, and the staff was working overtime to try and keep up with the demand. Working mandatory overtime for the past few weeks was beginning to take its toll on me and my staff, but it was worth it when we were able to complete the project on time. The day FedEx came and picked up the last box to be shipped to the CDC was the day that I took everyone out to celebrate our hard work and efforts.

Calling ahead and paying extra to get in without a reservation, we stepped into R. Kitchen as a large group and ordered our food before going outside onto the back patio. It was a warm evening in Charleston, and the city came alive with music and tourists. We could tell by the way everyone stared intently at the overhead menu that they weren't from the city and smiled politely as we sat and watched the sights.

"That last project was crazy, but I know my check is gonna look right when I get it!" Evan smiled as he rubbed his hands together. "We worked what, 'bout ten hours of OT this week?"

"Yea, 'bout ten hours." I frowned my face and calculated the time in my head. We'd all stayed an extra two hours after our regular hours to get the bonus promised to us by the lab in Georgia. I didn't tell my team about that; I wanted it to be a surprise in their paychecks. "Aye, thank y'all again for the team effort, I really appreciate it."

"Oh, no prob, boss lady," Lola spoke up first, and everyone agreed. "We appreciate your leadership above all; if it was somebody else, I would already be at home with my feet kicked up because I don't stay past work time for nobody."

"Oh yea, that last boss we had? Couldn't pay me all the deep wave wigs from Mayven to stay past 5 o'clock," Maurice chimed in. "Girl, I had a show to do one time and missed it messing around with that ass clown," he grumbled, picking his perfectly manicured hands.

The waitress brought our food out onto the patio, and we focused on getting our grub on. R. was known for allowing guest chefs to come in and prepare their traditional five course meals, and this night's meal was nothing short of amazing. After finishing up my ribeye steak, I went inside to thank the chef and had to stand in line; I wasn't the only one who enjoyed the food. Hearing the tone in the couple's voices behind me, I secretly hoped that the line would move a little quicker as the woman in front of me gushed about how the food didn't taste like that wherever they were from.

As the man behind me growled lowly, the woman with him stepped on my foot in an attempt to escape his accusations. Wincing in pain, I turned to face her, wearing my thoughts on my face. "My bad," she mumbled passively, turning back to him.

"Leonie, allow me to apologize for my friend's actions," Keyon's voice spoke as his strong, gentle hand landed on my shoulder.

"Your friend?" she raised her voice slightly, staring back and forth between us and taking note of his hand on me. "Since when did we become friends?"

"Mariah, not now," Keyon spoke through gritted teeth. "You just stepped on this woman's foot and didn't give her the common courtesy of an apology."

"I said 'my bad'; that's a pretty damn good apology, if you ask me." She rolled her eyes in my direction.

"Keyon, it's fine, really. I appreciate the gesture." I tried to minimize my pain in order to avoid making a scene.

"See? Fat bitch said it's fine. Now I wanna—" she started as he grabbed her by the elbow and ushered her out of the line before I opened my mouth.

Tristan was gone, but I got that same feeling in the pit of my stomach that I always got whenever he said that same disrespectful bullshit that this ghetto rat seemed to think was ok for her to say. I wasn't the only person in the restaurant with a few extra pounds; even the people behind me looked as if they were about to start a riot had Keyon not pulled her out of line. Shaking my head, I went back to the table to join my team, but my mind wasn't in it anymore. I was ready to go home and ball up underneath the sheets for the rest of the night.

"Boss lady, you ok?" Lola questioned when she saw me gathering my things.

"Yea, I'm fine." I flagged down the waitress for the check as they stared at me with concern. "I'll take care of the food; y'all stay and have fun. I don't feel well."

"Nuh-uh, what happened?" Maurice stood up and began looking around the restaurant wildly. "Who did it? I'm 'bout to go—"

"Y'all, for real, it's nothing. I'll be ok," I loved how overprotective they were of me. I was an only child, and not used to having anyone looking out for my well being. "I'll see you Monday, ok?"

"Ok," they all called out at the same time, watching me as I went to the register and paid for their food. Heading outside to my car, I saw Keyon and the lady parked two cars away from me and hurried to my vehicle before I changed my mind and walked over to introduce my fist to her front grill. Pulling my phone from my purse, I dialed Nyoka's number; we needed to talk.

"Leonie, what's wrong?" Nyoka's voice was urgent in my ear as I started up my car.

"Girl, I'm up here at—" I started, then stopped. Keyon got his little friend in the car and winked at me as he was circling around to the driver's side. "Aye Ny, lemme call you back."

Glancing quickly at her face scowling at the phone in her hand, I looked back at him as he held his fingers up to his face, signaling that he would call me later. Nodding my head, I smiled as he mouthed the words 'I'm sorry' before turning back to the car and lowering himself in. Normally I wouldn't have given him the time of day, but considering his date, I was a little curious.

Pulling off, my phone rang again halfway down the street. "Leonie, what the hell? Where are you?"

"I was about to call you and tell you about what happened at R. Kitchen with that one police officer, but never mind now." I rode with a smile on my face as I headed across the bridge to Mount Pleasant.

"Never mind? Leonie, if you don't—"

"Ok girl, you remember the police officer..." I began telling the story as I drove, not leaving anything out.

By the time I made it to my townhouse, we were in agreement about Keyon calling me later; under normal circumstances, she'd be trying to talk me out of it. Pulling up, I saw a car parked in front of my place, and he got out as I was pulling in my driveway. "Ny, I'll call you tomorrow, ok?"

"Mmhmm. Let me know everything too," she cheered before hanging up.

"I just came to apologize to you again for Mariah's actions," he began, walking next to me as we walked into the house together. "I don't tolerate that type of behavior from anybody in my space, much less somebody I'm dating."

"You can't control what people say," I replied, opening the door and stepping inside as he came in behind me, closing and locking the door. "But I appreciate your apology."

"No problem," he kicked off his shoes at the door and spoke. "Haven't seen you in a while, are you ok? What's the latest update with your boyfriend?"

"First of all, he's not my boyfriend," I began, heading to the kitchen to grab two bottles of water. "He's someone I used to date. Second, his trial starts in about two weeks, so I'll be at that."

"That's right, his trial is coming up on the docket. Did I tell you how proud I was of you for seeing this case through and not dropping the charges?" he spoke quietly as I sat down next to him, passing him the bottle.

We opened our drinks at the same time, and I fixated on his lips as he took a long, much needed pull from the bottle. Feeling my bottom lip slowly drop open, I enjoyed the scene in front of me: Charleston's sexiest police officer with some of the thickest lips wrapped sensually around a Deer Park water bottle, siphoning his fill and quenching his thirst. Allowing my mind to wander on the potential of what else those lips were capable of, I imagined myself wrapped up in those strong hands of his, melting into his arms in a pool of hormones and liquid lust. Closing my eyes, I took a deep breath and held it in, praying that I didn't jump this man's bones and thank him the right way for defending me earlier.

"Leonie?"

"Hmm? Oh... huh? You said something, Keyon?"

"I was asking you about the case, but I see your mind is elsewhere." I saw a small smile on his lips as he reached out a hand to brush my hair back from my face.

"No, I was just trying to think of the perfect response other than another 'thank you'," I replied as he leaned down and grabbed my foot, placing it carefully in his lap. Gently kneading all my sore spots in his manly hands, I allowed my head to roll back and relaxed on the back of the couch. All types of lewd thoughts ran through my mind as I took advantage of Keyon's foot massage.

"No need to thank me, love. A man is supposed to hold you up, pray for you, wipe your tears, and speak life into the beautiful woman that you are. I can tell from looking in your eyes that you've never had that, am I right?"

I nodded my head in response; the two men that I'd been with before tonight were nothing like what he was describing. I'd heard stories from my married friends about how their men empowered them to be the best woman ever, how they had that daily encouragement to walk in the path of purpose for their lives and envied them. And now... now, I had a man rubbing MY feet after he'd been fighting injustices on the streets of Charleston, telling me about how it was a man's job to uplift his better half.

"Keyon?"

"Yes, Leonie?"

"Can I... can I touch it?"

"Touch what, baby?"

"You know..." I dropped my eyes to the place where I prayed I could do more than touch. "It."

Following my eyes, he looked down at his growing erection and smiled. "As much as I want to say yes, I can't let you do that, baby."

"Why not?" I jumped up, snatching my foot from his grip. "Oh, I know. I'm bigger than you thought I was, so now you just trying to figure out a way to be nice so you can leave, ain't you?"

"Leonie, you are so far off that you don't even realize when a man doesn't want anything from you. You so blinded by what people have to say about your weight that you can't even see when somebody is really feeling you for more than just sex," he jumped up and yelled back.

"Keyon, get out of my house!" I screamed, embarrassed by his words and my actions. "And don't come back!" I yelled, slamming the door in his face.

"I'll call you tomorrow!" I heard his voice on the other side of my door as it echoed through my neighborhood. Peeking through the curtains, I saw him snatch the door to his car open and slam it closed before he peeled off down the street.

Shit.

∞

True to his word, Keyon called me the next day, but I ignored his call. I was so embarrassed at my actions and his response; I couldn't believe I asked him to let me touch his private parts, albeit impressive. The fact that he was a gentleman about the situation had me perplexed; any other man would've jumped at the chance to have a woman stroking his... wait. I should be thankful that he turned me down, considering the circumstances; if the shoe was on the other foot, I know I would've reacted completely differently. I had to apologize to him, but how?

Either way it went, it was Valentine's Day and I didn't have any plans. Busying myself around the house, I turned on some music and started cleaning up my place to take my mind off the fact that it was the most romantic day of the year that I'd be spending, once again, with myself. I bought my townhouse a few years ago and was amazed at how much stuff piled up in the guest bedroom and my study. I was finally at that stage mentally where I could collect Tristan's things into a central area and have Keyon drop them off at his house.

Keyon…touching my face with my fingertips, I trembled at the memory of last night before I said what I said. His fingers on my skin… for the first time, I felt completely at ease when in the room with a man and wanted to give myself to him completely. Tristan never stirred the feelings in me that Keyon did, yet we'd been together for six months. My hair rose on the back of my neck when he reached down and grabbed my foot; I craved that same touch even now after I put him out of my place. I wanted him back. I wanted him back NOW.

My doorbell rang and brought me out of my daydream. Ny said she'd be stopping by to find out what happened between me and Keyon last night, so I headed to the door with my hair up in a messy bun, an old t-shirt and some jogging pants.

"Girl, thanks for coming over. I messed last night up so bad I don't think that man will ever talk to me again," I spoke, opening the door and turning back to my cleaning.

"I don't know about ever," I heard Keyon's voice behind me as his footsteps walked in and the door closed. "I think he knows that you've had your share of clowns, so it's gonna take some time for you to let your guard down and let a man love the woman that you are."

"Boy, what you doing at my house!" I yelled, putting my hand across my chest, ready to run upstairs to put on my face and change clothes. At the very least, I needed to put on a bra. He grabbed me in the middle of my escape and we stood silently, sharing each other's space. Faintly, I heard the music blaring in the background, his lips nuzzled against my ear.

"Honestly? Showing you what a relationship looks like. I thought about you all night, Leonie. Thought about what I could do to show you what couple excellence should be; if you fell for a Tristan, apparently you don't know. A true relationship, love, is two imperfect people not giving up on each other. Make no mistake, baby, I promise that no matter how much you push me away, I'll never give up on you, Leonie."

"Why me though, Keyon? What is it that you see in me that makes you say that? We barely know each other."

"I ain't gonna lie, I've played the field. Women love a man in uniform. I see the beauty in your soul, your heart. I want the opportunity to make you believe in love and happily ever after again. I don't give a damn about your weight, your past, none of that. If you follow my lead, I can be all you need. I want you to trust me, Leonie. Can you trust me with your heart, can you trust me with you?"

Part of me wanted to say yes. I wanted so badly to say yes so that this mahogany burnished Adonis could restore my faith in the art of love, restore my hope in the chase and the ultimate prize: marriage. But I couldn't. I'd always been told that I should marry my best friend, and although me and Keyon were cool, we hadn't achieved that level of comfort with one another just yet. Admitting that to myself was one thing, saying it out loud was made it official.

"Keyon, I can't."

He was crushed, and I wanted nothing more than to take my words back, rewind the moment and say yes. With Tristan, it was easy. I didn't understand why with Keyon, it was so hard.

"You know what? I understand, Leonie. I do. Sometimes you can sabotage what could be a beautiful life for yourself by thinking that it's too good to be true. Your mind can play tricks on you, tell you that you don't deserve to be happy. But I made you a promise. If that promise takes the rest of my life for me to bring to fruition… Leonie, I'm here for the long haul. You not gonna get rid of me that easy."

Chapter 5

Two years ago

"What about him?" Nyoka asked as she twirled the umbrella in her drink.

"Him?" I turned my nose up as the man swiveled his hips faster than a stripper on a good Saturday night as he walked past us. "Nah, I think we looking for the same thing," I snickered.

"What about him?" She pointed at a sexy chocolate brother with a chest that made me want to lick his left pectoral.

"Yea, he'll do." I licked my lips as he headed in our direction. *Did he read my mind?* I wondered as he closed the space between us. Something about his smile was familiar to me, but I couldn't put my finger on why.

"Hello, Leonie. Long time no see," Keyon spoke as he sat down next to me, signaling for the bartender to bring us another round. "How have you been?"

Ninety degrees in the Bahamas, and this man still gave me the chills. "I'm ok. How have you been?" I asked as a slim, caramel-skinned woman eased up behind him and wrapped her arms around his neck.

"Good. I've been pretty good myself," he replied, unwrapping the woman's arms to introduce her. "Leonie, this is my fiancée, Jenessé. Jenessé, this is Leonie, a good friend of mine."

"Good friend, huh?" she questioned, staring me up and down until she was satisfied he was telling the truth. "Nice meeting you," she spoke dismissively, waving me off. "Keyon, I wanna go get in the pool."

"Ok, here I come," he replied, not moving an inch.

"Now, Keyon," she whined. "I wanna go now, baby."

"I'll catch up with you later, Leonie," Keyon replied, giving in to her whiny demands while dropping the money for our refills on the bar. He didn't seem like the type that would go for that type of woman, but looks can be deceiving.

"Mmmph, who was THAT!" Nyoka purred as we both turned to watch him walk away. "You never told me about him, Leonie!"

"There wasn't anything to tell, really. Remember the police officer I told you about when me and Tristan fell out last year?"

"Ol' fraud life Tris? Yea, I remember him. That's the police officer, though?"

"Yea girl."

"Hmph, I wouldn't have let that get away hunny," she lectured as I watched Jenessé wrap her arm around his waist as if she was marking her territory. *Keyon must've told her about me and now the bitch sees me as a threat,* I thought as she turned around and locked eyes with me. I rolled mine at her and turned back around to finish my drink.

He promised... Keyon promised me that he was there for the long haul. Yes, I might've shut him out to figure out exactly what I wanted, but he assured me that he would bring that promise to fruition if it took the rest of our lives. Yet, here he was, a year to the day later on a Valentine's Day singles' cruise with his fiancée. His fiancée. She wasn't even cute; I'm sure she was running around here telling people those buck teeth in her mouth were an overbite. Ol' bad body having, stick figure looking like a Chia Pet done snagged her a police officer, then had the nerve to look me up and down with her nose turned so far up I could read her thoughts.

"Earth to Leonie." Ny snapped her fingers in my face, blinking me back to the present. "Where did you go just then?"

"I guess I wasn't as over Tristan as I thought I was," I lied. I was over Tristan the day he stole my BMW and parked it in front of the house he shared with his common-law wife. I saw that case all the way through to the end; sat in court in the front row every time he went and made sure he got jail time. In my opinion, James could be as hobosapien as he wanted to be with three hots and a cot. No, the person who held my attention had a whiny cunt attached to his waist, and I was in the middle of figuring out a way to unwrap her bony arms from around my man. See, what Keyon's little fiancée didn't know was that her man liked his women with a little cellulite.

"Well, when we touch down in Jamaica, you'll be saying, 'Tristan? What the hell is a Tristan?'" she giggled as we clanked our drinks.

"Why? You hooking me up with one of your sexy relatives?" I asked as I took a sip of my Bahama Mama.

"No," she spoke slyly. "We're not going to my family home. As a matter of fact, they don't even know I'm here."

"They don't?" Originally from the islands, Ny told me that once we docked, we would be staying with her Aunt Ruthie, so I didn't need to book a hotel room. "So, where are we staying?"

"Well it was supposed to be a surprise," she began, taking a sip from her drink before smiling at me slyly.

"A surprise? Ny, tell me where we're staying for the next two nights?"

"Hedonism."

My eyes bucked out of their sockets as my mouth dropped open. "Hedonism?"

Ny nodded her head up and down, giving me a sneaky grin. "First box of condoms is on me; after that, you're on your own," she said, spoken like a true doctor. I had to mentally prepare myself for two days of no holds barred, anything goes, H-E-D-O-N-I-S-M!

No matter how much trash I talked, I was still a little hesitant about participating in hedonism with Ny. First and foremost, ever since that incident with Tristan— damn, I mean James— I was hesitant about trusting anyone at the gym anymore, women included. So, I stopped going, choosing to buy a few workout videos and some weights to maintain my figure that way. I firmed up in some areas, but in my opinion, I still had a long way to go.

Second, I had only been with two people sexually in my entire life, and neither of those were experiences that I chose to keep burned in my memory. I didn't think of myself as an expert by any means; the thought of hedonism itself scared the shit out of me. What if I did something wrong? What if Tristan was lying when he said that I sucked a mean dick? I didn't want to be the butt of some stranger's jokes for the rest of my life when he retold the story to his favorite cousins and frat brothers about what happened 'that one time he went to hedonism.'

"Maybe I'll just stay here in the room. You can go and have a good time," I said as I watched Ny get ready for a night of debauchery in Jamaica.

"No, the whole point behind us coming was so you can get your groove back, so put on some lace panties, a push up bra, and come on Stella!" she snickered, grabbing my arm and smacking me on my butt playfully.

"Ny, I just don't think—"

"That's the beauty of it, you don't have to overthink it. Just go and have fun. That's what hedonism is all about, Leonie, releasing your inhibitions. Girl, stop worrying about your size; there are people there that are bigger than you. Go show off that sexy body of yours!"

"I guess, Ny. But, if I don't like it, I'm coming back to the room with or without you."

"Something tells me that I might beat you back to the room tonight," she whispered under her breath.

"What did you say?"

"I said go and get your back arched tonight. Come on, we're gonna be late."

I went and got ready, quickly jumping in the shower and getting clean. "Late? For a sex party? They got the nerve to have a specific time frame?" I sighed as I walked out the bathroom, pulling my hair back into a ponytail and securing it with a rubber band at the nape of my neck.

"Girl," Ny began as the waterworks started. "You look beautiful," she gushed.

"Do I?" I took her advice; once I stepped out of the shower, I rubbed myself down with some rose oil and threw on a black lace push-up bra with matching boy shorts. I wasn't the same size I was last year; I guess I must've managed to tone in just the right places. Applying a touch of foundation and giving myself a smoky eye, I finished my look with a pop of lip gloss. Walking back into the suite to grab my matching sheer robe and kitten heels, I hadn't paid any attention to my overall appearance.

"Come on, girl, before I change my mind and keep you in this suite all to myself. You know I ain't never went that route, but you might make me change my mind tonight!" she cheered as we grabbed our room keys and headed downstairs to catch the shuttle to the other side of the island for the festivities.

∞

Stepping off the shuttle, I thought I would see people all over the place just fucking everywhere; on the ground, in the bushes, on the trees. To my surprise, it was quiet.

"In case we get separated, this is the spot that the shuttle will pick you up from. The vans run every hour and a half, so if you miss one, you know how long you'll have to stand here waiting for another." Giving me a quick hug and a peck on the cheek, she disappeared into the darkness.

I stood around awkwardly, waiting on something to happen. Finally, I got tired and decided to go find somewhere that I could rest my legs and maybe find something to drink. As I walked through the woods, a strong hand reached out and grabbed me. I was about to scream when I felt a pair of soft, manly lips pressed against mine. Remembering where I was and why I was there, I tried to relax, but my mind wouldn't allow me to. The stranger stopped, and after some fumbling, held a bottle to my lips.

Against my better judgment, I took a drink, allowing the smooth, sweet liquid to caress my throat and quench my thirst. The stranger then pressed his lips against mine for a second time and I allowed him inside of my mouth; our tongues dipped in and out of each other's lips as if we were lovers reunited after years of being apart. He reached around and palmed my round apple bottom, squeezing my cheeks tightly as he lifted me up so that my pussy rested against his manhood. Wrapping my legs around his waist, he pinned me up against the tree and grinded on my sex; I felt his thick, pulsating cock as it throbbed against the thin material holding it hostage.

"You feel that?" he whispered in my ear, his words laden with longing, not missing a stroke.

"Yes," I responded breathlessly, ready for whatever was about to happen. "I feel that."

"Can I put him inside of you? Please?"

"Mmhmm," I moaned, feeling my own juices as they pooled at my opening, anxiously awaiting his arrival.

Snatching his pants down with one hand, he grabbed his dick with urgency and shoved it inside of me, spreading me wide open to the hilt. Biting my lip, I wanted to scream, but all that escaped me was a yearning whimper as he took his time gliding in and out of my sopping pussy. Raising my arms up over my head, he held me in place with one hand as his other hand snatched my bra off and tickled my nipples between his teeth, making me want him even more.

"Ssssshh," I hissed as I felt myself rain on his thick erection.

"You feel so fucking good," his raspy whisper breathed in my ear. "That pussy so fucking wet and juicy, damn!"

I couldn't even respond; my pussy was going into convulsions for the third time since he slid inside of me. I was loving every stroke, every pump; every entrance was harder than the one before, and it had me close to speaking in tongues! Matching his stroke, I thrust my hips forward when he retreated, and he returned the favor over and over as the bark from the tree dug in my back with a pain that I deemed necessary to bring me pleasure. The fragrant flowers indigenous to the island made me slightly dizzy as I watched him throw his head back; I bit his neck as he pounded me harder and harder. He impaled me on the tree as I tasted his blood mixed with his sweat salty in my mouth, moving my head downward to lick his strong, broad chest as we both came together.

Feeling him still semi erect after he emptied his seed on the ground and rested his manhood against my pussy lips, I vaguely remembered the condoms Ny gave me earlier that I left in my hotel room. Never had a man made love to me like this man did; before tonight I had yet to experience the chills as they overtook my body in the sweltering Jamaican heat.

The stranger dropped to his knees and sucked my pussy as if it was his last meal; twirling his tongue around my clit before working his way inside of me slowly, like a caterpillar. He would then lap at my pearl, slowly building up his pace with fervor until my clit felt rigid against his tongue, then slow back down as if he was taking his time to ensure my enjoyment. Grabbing the back of his head, I tried to pump his face, but he would move so that I understood that he was in control. I gave up, allowing him the lead, and he brought me back to the edge of our own personal cliff of passion before standing up quickly and sliding back inside of my thick thighs as I fell off into an exuberant free fall of seduction.

We went on like that for most of the night; nothing mattered but me, him, and that patch of dirt somewhere on the island of Jamaica. As the sun peeked from behind the ocean, he whispered in my ear that the last shuttle would be coming soon, and I needed to make my way back to the pickup spot. I heeded his advice, grabbing my sheer coverup and allowing him to escort me to the road. When the doors closed behind me, I saw his figure waving goodbye and I returned the gesture. At that point, it hit me: I never saw his face.

Chapter 6

Ny tried to convince me to go back with her on the second night of our trip, but after the night I had, I was good. Not only did I have sex with a random stranger whose face I never saw, but I also allowed him to cum inside of me NUMEROUS times. I had to report to the nearest drug store as soon as I stepped off the boat in Miami; damn that 'waiting until I got back to Charleston' mess.

Despite my whorish behavior, that night left me in a languid mood. For the remainder of our trip on the island, I felt a release unlike any other; this time, I felt liberated. The world was at my fingertips; I felt like anything was possible. Ny and I went shopping, and I picked up a few souvenirs for friends. I grabbed my mother a few dresses to wear around the house while she cooked and cleaned. I felt so good, I even grabbed my boss a few shot glasses, even though he didn't drink. Maybe he'd get the hint.

On the trip back across the Caribbean, I didn't see Keyon and his 'fiancée' again, but it wasn't from a lack of effort on my part. I WANTED to bump into her again, and dare her to give me that same stank look that she did before. The type of mood I was in, she might've found herself at the bottom of the ocean.

With my little detour to CVS, we barely made it to the airport in time for our flight back home, and I slept the entire flight. As we were standing in the middle of the parking structure at the airport, trying to remember where we parked once we got back to Charleston, I accidentally bumped into a silver Challenger with chrome wheels and tinted windows. Thinking no one was in the car, imagine my surprise when the window rolled down and Keyon was staring me in the face with a smile.

"What a coincidence. You need a ride to your car?"

Ny almost knocked me over with a resounding 'YES', but there was something about Keyon that changed since we saw him on the boat.

"So, uhm, where's Jenessé?" I inquired innocently, sliding in his car on the passenger side as Ny hopped in the back seat.

"She needed some more time," he replied nonchalantly as we circled the parking structure.

"Oh."

Knowing that he and his fiancée broke up and seeing the fresh bite mark on the side of his neck, my heart told me that I wouldn't be taking the morning after pill in my purse after all.

∞

"I— I can't come in today, Rob," I whimpered in the phone after my second breakfast made its way out of my mouth and into the toilet. "I feel horrible."

"Maybe it was something you ate," he spoke gently as I felt something travel up my esophagus. Allowing the liquid the release it deserved, I turned my attention back to the phone.

"You're right. As soon as I stop throwing up, I'm going to—" I started and stopped, feeling another wave coming on.

"I get it, Leonie. Take all the time you need; just keep me informed, ok?"

"Ok." I threw the phone down, hoping it hung up on its own because I wasn't the one today.

Just as I suspected, that night in Jamaica with who I hoped was Keyon left me pregnant with someone's baby. It probably wasn't even him. If it was, why hadn't he called? My number hadn't changed. I waited three weeks for him to get in contact with me and say something… anything that confirmed that it was him that night, and nothing. It was too late for me to take the morning after pill, and I didn't believe in abortion. My plan was to have the baby and give him or her up for adoption; I didn't aspire to be a single parent.

Hearing my phone ring as I choked down a spoonful of baking soda, courtesy of my mother's down home remedies, I grabbed it at the fourth ring.

"Oh, honey; I called as soon as I heard!" Ny's voice soothed my borderline mental breakdown over my situation. "Are you ok? Do you want me to bring you anything?"

"Yea, can you find my baby's father and tell him to call me?" I spoke wearily into the phone's speaker.

"Your baby's father?" she questioned. "Leonie, are you pregnant?" My silence spoke volumes; I heard her suck in her breath and blow it out. "Please don't tell me you got pregnant from the weekend we spent in Jamaica? Leonie, you had the Plan B! Why didn't you take it?"

"I don't know, Ny!" I broke down in tears. "I don't know!"

"What are you going to do, sweetie? I know you're not thinking about—"

"Don't say it, Ny, because I'm not. I'm going to give him or her to a loving home where he or she will be well taken care of," I sniffed, wiping my face.

"Oh Leonie, I'm here for you. Whatever you decide to do, I'm right here."

"Thanks, Ny. You've always been a great friend. Can you bring me some soup when you get off work today?"

"Of course I can. Anything else?"

"Jell-O," I burped as an after effect from the baking soda.

"Jell-O it is. See you later, Leonie."

"Ok Ny." My mood brightened a little as I hung up the phone. *I guess it's gonna be me, Mama, and Ny getting me through these nine months,* I thought to myself as I started cleaning up.

Keyon's words to me about sabotaging what could be a beautiful life for myself by thinking that it's too good to be true haunted me in my quiet hours. The stranger's lips on my secret places were those same lips I saw in my dreams every night. Soft pecks on my inner thighs from my island trip were more than just sex; in his touch, I felt his true intentions. I felt the same way during those brief conversations that we had in the past year; Keyon always called me to check up on my well-being, even if it was between his evening tours as a police officer. He called me to see how my day was going and on the days we didn't talk, he always responded to my text messages. He would ask about how work was going, celebrate my accomplishments at work as the most efficient lab manager in South Carolina, and even sent me a bouquet of roses when the lab won a regional award for patient service and excellence. How he knew we were nominated was beyond me, but I sent him a thank you text anyway.

At the end of the day, though, Keyon wasn't my Prince Charming. The fact remained that he was on a cruise with his fiancée, a skinny bitch by the name of Jenessé. When he introduced her to me, I knew that there was something that he'd told her about me; why else would she react like that if he told her we were just friends?

I couldn't get that night out of my mind, though; yes, my mind told me that the stranger was Keyon, but if it wasn't, whoever it was still rocked my world. Twisting me in positions that I'd never been in, touching me using mainly his lips and tongue as he pleasured my body in ways that I've never experienced… that night, my weight was the last thing on my mind. The stranger was going for complete satisfaction and ultimate control of my mind, body and soul, and that's what he got. I closed my eyes and felt his gentle strokes in my sleep, woke up moaning and engulfed in lust more than once since my trip. I had to know who held more command over my body than I; whose touch was forever a part of my memories, forever a part of me. Who was the father of my unborn child?

Damn, I hope it's Keyon. Mmm… I hope it's Keyon…

∞

My boss gave me a few days off, so I figured I'd stop by the library to check out a few books to cuddle up with. After talking to the librarian at the local branch in Mount Pleasant and finding out they had no urban fiction section, I headed across the bridge to the main library in Charleston to see if I could find the book Ny was telling me about the other day. She was reading part two of a series about these four men from Wilmington, Delaware whose wives took them through all types of crazy. Secret kids, pedophile relatives that were low-key crazy, baby mama drama… and that was all while they were still dating. On top of that, one of 'em was a snake. I think she said it was by Fatima Munroe.

"Hey, Ms. Miller," Ms. Dorinda, the librarian, called out softly as I walked up to the research desk. "What brings you by today?"

"Haven't seen you at the lab lately," I responded, fingering the magazines on the desk. "It looks a mess without you there keeping us on our toes." Dorinda worked part-time at the lab on the weekends cleaning up the office. She didn't have access to the back offices; just the front reception area and the bathrooms. We weren't messy, but I loved the smell of bleach and lavender Comet first thing Monday morning after she cleaned.

"Been spending time with these grandkids of mine; they keep me on my toes," she smiled and adjusted the clear frames on her face. "My daughter paid for us to go to Atlantic City these past two weeks and..." I nodded politely and smiled here and there as she told me about her vacation. Ms. Dorinda didn't have to work; she had a beautiful pension from the school system and worked purely to keep herself busy. "Enough about me; you didn't answer my question, honey. What brings you by today?"

"I'm looking for a book by Fatima Munroe; I think it's called *Boss Status-Loving A Street King*? Do you have it here?"

"Lemme go check," she responded, turning to the computer to look up the author's name. "Munroe... Munroe... here it is. She must be pretty popular; you're the third person that's been in here looking for her books."

"New author, who dis?" I giggled. "Nah, she been writing for a while. I heard about her from one of my friends; if I know Ny, she probably telling half of Charleston about that book. Plus, I like to support women authors as much as possible, you know?"

"Me too. I might have to grab one of her books too, just to see what the fuss is about," she gushed heartily.

"Uhmm... Ms. Dorinda, Ny told me she got a few sex scenes in that book that you might not wanna—"

"Girl, I know about sex. I got kids; they didn't get here because we sat on the porch and stared at each other like they do in the movies. Hunny, the stories I could—"

"Bye, Ms. Dorinda." I hurried to the shelves where their urban books were kept before she told me a story that I was positive I didn't need the mental image burned in my memory from. Finding what I needed, along with Jahquel J.'s *B.A.E.* series, I checked out my books and waved goodbye to the librarian. As soon as I stepped outside, I realized I wasn't ready to go home just yet, so I walked down to the aquarium on the water's edge to get some fresh air and my daily exercise. I loved hearing the water as it lapped at the shore, giving me the peace and tranquility that I longed for; considering my world had already been turned upside down.

Listening to the ocean's waves in the background, I was all into Troy and Love's story from *Boss Status* when I heard a commotion behind me. Standing up when my ears picked up a woman screaming, I heard footsteps coming up behind me quickly, almost as if someone was running— WHAM! Someone collided with me hard, sending my books flying one way while I hit the ground.

"HE STOLE MY PURSE!" she screamed as the body collected itself. Jumping up quickly, he/she/it took off with BOTH of our bags; mine and the woman's. Hesitating for a second to process what just happened, I joined her and screamed too; my prenatal vitamins were in that bag.

"HELP!" we both cried out in unison as the police cruiser sped to where we both stood crying out in anguish. The first officer jumped out of the driver's side while the second one took off running behind the thief. While the woman explained her story to the officer, I watched as the second man quickly eliminated the space between him and the criminal before tackling him to the ground and handcuffing him. Call me horny, but he had a nice ass.

The woman was being super extra; by now, she was crying alligator tears and mopping her face with the older officer's handkerchief that he handed her out of sympathy. "I—I don't understand why he would do that," she bawled in the middle of the boardwalk.

Ignoring her, I turned my attention back to the officer who was snatching the man in cuffs back and forth as he popped him a few times in the back of his head.

"Go get you a job or a trade; snatching purses ain't gonna get you shit but jail time. You wanna be on the yard with murderers and dope boys talking 'bout how you got locked up for snatching purses? They gonna tag that ass, booty boy. You want these big, grown men calling you booty boy for the next five years?" he teased, smacking the boy's head and the back of his neck a few more times. The thief wasn't any older than about seventeen, at the good. "By the way, they don't just say it, they gonna get in that ass, booty boy," he boomed.

"Keyon?"

"You know who that is, booty boy?" He smacked the boy's head again. "That's my girl. You stealing from my girl, booty boy?"

"I didn't—" the boy pleaded, but Keyon cut him off.

"Looka here, booty boy. If you ever, EVER see this face again and THINK about taking ANYTHING from HER? Anything from this one right here?" He pointed in my direction, "I'll see to it that you do a mandatory life sentence, even if I gotta make some charges stick, feel me?"

"Yes, sir," the boy shook with fear at his threat.

"Now, apologize to my boo and this woman for fucking up their day." He shoved him in our direction and stood patiently.

"Ma'am? I'm sorry, ma'am."

"Tell her what you sorry for, booty boy. Tell both of them what you sorry for."

"Sorry for stealing your purses."

"And?" Keyon gripped him forcefully around his neck as the older white lady looked on approvingly.

"Sor— sorry for fucking up your day, ma'am," he mumbled.

"They didn't hear you." Keyon yanked him back and forth again.

"SORRY FOR FUCKING UP YOUR DAY, MA'AM!"

"That's better. Now, take your meth smoking ass somewhere and jump off a bridge," he pushed him to the ground and stepped over his crumpled body. The boy jumped up and took off running in the opposite direction as the officers laughed.

"Booty boy, Officer Braithwaite?" the first officer turned and asked... my man, I guess?

"His ass liked that shit. You see the look on his face?" Keyon joked. "He was 100% ready for me to throw him in the back of the car!"

"Thank you so much, officers. Thank you," the old lady expressed her gratitude to both officers for their actions. I, on the other hand, wasn't impressed by nothing but Keyon's backside.

"So, you must be Chief Watson's daughter, huh?" the first officer tipped his hat to me before reaching out to shake my hand. "Nice to meet you, your father is a great man."

Keyon shook his head behind me as I watched the older white lady walk off down the boardwalk; my mind wondering why he would think I was related to Charleston's chief of police. "Nice meeting you too. By the way, no, I'm not Chief Watson's daughter. See you around, Keyon," I headed back to the bench to grab my library books, leaving Keyon to explain to his co-worker how he managed to have a fiancée and a girlfriend, yet neither of us had a pot of hot grits waiting on the stove for him.

"What you got goin' on with that one, Braithwaite? You gonna give it all up for her?"

"That's wife type, I'm ready to throw rice on it, feel me?" Keyon's words drifted back to me on the ocean breeze.

Hmph. Throwing rice, yet you still engaged. How, Keyon? How?

Chapter 7

A little over a year ago

I was nine months pregnant, and ready to get this whole thing over with. After the first month, my body acclimated to the life growing inside of me, and I had no issues. Ny hooked me up with the best OB/GYN in Charleston, and I liked his bedside manner. Skyler was handsome, gentle with me, and understood my position. Our relationship progressed from a doctor/patient one to taking it one day at a time and seeing where it went. He knew where I stood regarding my pregnancy and didn't judge me for my decision, nor did he try to talk me out of it. Just like Ny, he was in my corner with whatever I ultimately decided to do.

I contacted an agency and flipped through at least a million profiles before I decided on a nice couple in California to adopt my baby boy. The husband worked in Silicon Valley while the wife was a stay at home wife and hopeful parent. They agreed to an open adoption; I wanted to see what my first son looked like and in case he decided to look for me, I wanted him to have my number. The only thing I regretted was that if he asked about his father, I wouldn't be able to give him any information. I had sex with a ghost one night in Jamaica, which produced a child.

It was the last day before I went on maternity leave, per my doctor's orders. Faith and Jacobi were flying to Charleston tomorrow, and would be at the hospital when I was induced in a few days. My co-workers threw me a baby shower at the lab, and it seemed like every doctor and lab tech in the hospital showed up to drop off gifts and cards. My truck was full of baby items that I would be dropping off at the Salvation Army; the only people that knew I wasn't keeping the baby were Ny and Skyler.

Just as one of the techs from my office loaded the stroller into the back of my new Jeep Cherokee, a police cruiser circled the lot and stopped on the side of my truck. "Need some help?" he asked my employee.

"No, we're good," Don called out as he closed the hatch. "Just making sure my boss is safe."

"I see. Aye, does Leonie still work here?" the officer asked.

"Last I checked, I'm still here," I spoke up haughtily and turned to look in the eyes of the man whose eyes, lips, and smile I saw in my dreams constantly. "Keyon?"

"You gonna be ok, Leonie?" Don asked with his hand on my shoulder, concern etched across his face.

"Yea, yea, I'll be fine." I waved him off as Keyon got out of his vehicle. "Lock up the lab for me, ok?"

"Ok," he called over his shoulder, jogging back inside.

"Leonie, what's all this? You pregnant?" he questioned, rubbing my swollen belly lovingly.

"Uhm, yea," I replied, unwillingly moving away from his touch.

"How many months?"

"Any day now, actually." I turned my face away in shame.

"Really. I didn't know you were pregnant. Your husband must be proud," I heard the acrimony in his tone.

"I'm not married."

"Not married?" I turned my face to catch the puzzled look on his slightly weathered face. "Boyfriend?"

"No."

"How many months did you say you were?"

"I didn't, but I'm 40 weeks."

Keyon tried counting on his fingers, but quickly gave up after a few seconds. "What's that in months?" he questioned genuinely.

"Nine and a half months," I laughed with him.

The wheels in his heads were turning quickly, I could see the calendar flipping backwards in his head. "Wait, you were pregnant when you and Ny went on the cruise?"

"I wasn't pregnant when I left the States, but apparently, when I got back I was," I replied bitterly.

Keyon stepped closer to me, his cologne swirling heavily in the air between us, inadvertently pulling us dangerously close together. Wrapping his arms around my growing waistline, he eliminated the small separation between us, his chest beckoning me to rest my head on it, and I did. His pectorals were so comforting to my skin; I closed my eyes and was immediately taken back to that night on the island when— wait.

"Did you enjoy yourself that night, baby?" he questioned, reading my mind as I realized that my initial assumptions were correct; it WAS him.

"I did," I whispered, my body suddenly shivering as a cool breeze blew up my skirt.

"I'm sorry, Leonie. I'm so sorry that I never told you," Keyon whispered as he peck kissed my head. "I've thought about you ever since that night, and I wanted to say something to you before now, but I didn't want—"

"You didn't want to be bothered with a big girl like me, huh." I wept as I pushed him away from me, the meaning of his words and what wasn't said cut through me like a knife. Men like Keyon were created for women like Jenessé, not me.

"I didn't want you to reject me once you found out my true identity," Keyon stared me in my eyes. "Look at you, Leonie. You're smart, sexy. A manager on your job. I ain't shit but a public servant; what can I give you on a policeman's salary that you can't do for yourself?"

"And Jenessé is a better fit for you?"

"Jenessé's father is the chief of police, what else could I do, Leonie? The boss tells you to date his daughter, she falls in love with you, next thing you know, someone's handing you an engagement ring telling you that you're getting married in a couple of months?" his voice pitched each time he spoke.

"Ooooh, I get it now. Not only would I need to be related to the chief of police, but I would also need to be about a hundred pounds lighter," I seethed, throwing my hands up in the air as he shook his head. "So, are you married now?" I asked, my bottom lip quivering as I waited for his answer with baited breath.

"Leonie, let me explain—"

"Just answer me that, Keyon," I interrupted. We were way past explaining; I was going to be induced in a few days. "Are you married now?"

"Yes. Yes, we got married—"

I broke down in tears; finding out that the man I was not just in love with, but also pregnant by was married to someone else? My heart couldn't take it, my soul couldn't handle it. Even though the adoption plans were in place, it wasn't final until the paperwork was complete. A part of me wanted to keep the baby, but I selfishly didn't want to do it alone.

"Leave me alone, Keyon!" I screamed, trying to grab my keys through my tears as I grasped aimlessly at my door handle.

"Leonie, wait! We still have to discuss my baby!"

"This ain't your baby, Keyon! This ain't even my baby! I'm giving him up to two people that are married to each other, that actually love and care about each other! Not two people that fucked one night at Hedonism! Leave me alone!" I cried, finally getting the door to my truck open.

Taking a minute to finish crying on my steering wheel, I sobbed loudly as Keyon beat on the window, begging me to open the door. I started up my car and blasted the radio to drown out his voice, wiping my eyes so I could pull out of the lot and get on with my life. Driving across the bridge, I broke down again with the realization that although we weren't officially in a relationship, Keyon broke my heart.

∞

I was in full nesting mode when I walked through Marshalls the next day and headed to their baby section. Damn, I wished me and Keyon would've worked out; they had some of the cutest little baby clothes. I would've spent all day dressing and undressing my baby in Ralph Lauren and Carter Baby onesies.

"Look at this one right here, bae," a voice tap danced on the nerve in my head that irritated me the most. "Ooo, I can't wait until we start a family together!"

"Sure, Jenessé. Whatever you say." I heard HIS voice with HERS. Peeking around the corner, I saw Keyon and Jenessé two aisles over; her looking every bit of her overbearing self while he looked like he had something better to do. "Are we done here?"

"Keyon, stop playing now, I'm being serious."

"So am I. Are we done here?"

"Sometimes, I wonder why you married me," she sighed, throwing a mini tantrum. That wasn't cute on her with them buck teeth; she really needed to figure out another way to catch her husband's attention.

"I'll tell you why. I respect your father a lot; even if he wasn't the chief of police, I'd still do whatever he asks. He asked me to date you, I did as a favor to him. You told him how much you wanted to be married, he pulled me to the side and told me he was dying and wanted to see you walk down the aisle as his last wish, I made it happen. Now, suddenly his condition isn't terminal, and I'm stuck with you. Still wondering?" he spoke in a low growl, and not a sexy one either.

"Why would you say something so ugly to me?"

"I didn't want you to go through this marriage confused. Are we done here or not?"

"Keyon, tell me you don't love me, and I promise I'll leave you alone," she begged in the middle of the store while gripping his jacket.

"You want the truth?"

"Yes."

"I'm in love with the mother of my child, but she— shit. It's complicated. This whole fucking thing is complicated." He ran his hands down his face while sighing deeply.

"I knew you was just talking, Keyon, you don't have a child," she waved him off, walking to HomeGoods with her phone stuck to her face. "Charleston ain't that big; I know all of your exes." I wonder which of his exes she thought left their teeth mark as a permanent tattoo on the side of his neck.

He walked quickly behind her with his hands in the air, ready to wring her neck before remembering he was in public. Turning his eyes skyward, I saw his lips move as he pleaded with Jesus for this woman to walk in front of a truck. I didn't know if that's what he was saying for real, but considering what he had to deal with, if I was him, I would be. Hurrying to the nearest exit, I scurried out of the store as quickly as I could at nine months pregnant before he saw me and made their argument any worse than what it was.

Keyon told his wife he loved me; I was feeling all warm and gushy inside. Maybe it was the hormones; knowing I was pregnant with his child and he loved me made me feel like an ass for all the times I purposely pushed him away. Now that I thought about it, I was kinda stupid for allowing another woman to come in and take my happiness. I was even more upset at the people who told me my whole life how I would never have anyone because of my weight.

Once I settled into my career, I would've thought that people would grow the fuck up, but apparently Jenessé and Marion, Keyon's ex, were stuck permanently with that childish mentality that would never get them far in life. Hell, Jenessé's father had to trick someone into marrying his daughter. I could lose the weight if I put my mind to it, but her grown ass would forever look like Bugs Bunny with those chapped lips and beaver fronts. Then, had the nerve to try and talk about my weight when she wasn't no better than me. Yankee Stadium didn't have enough seats for that bitch to have; she needed something more global.

It was time for me to glow up. My OB/GYN told me that my body would be healed fully in six weeks, and I was gonna use that time to work on a meal plan and exercising for real. I was gonna be slim thick in a matter of months and by then, I would be ready for whoever was destined to be in my life. God knows I would love for it to be Officer Keyon Braithwaite, but if it wasn't, I had to be in a position to accept the love given to me, however it manifested in my life.

Opening the door to my Jeep Cherokee, I felt my phone vibrate in my purse. Pulling the phone out of the side pocket, I slid the button to the right and hit answer as I closed my door.

"Leonie, where are you?" Keyon's voice was urgent, yet concerned in my ear. "We need to talk, for real."

"Keyon, I'm—" I started, then stopped. "Oh my God."

"What's wrong, baby?"

"Keyon, I gotta call you right back, ok?" I started crying; this couldn't be happening here of all places. *Not now... please not now...*

"Why Leonie? What's wrong?"

"I think my water just broke." I hung up in his face and dialed 911.

Chapter 8

"You're doing great, Leonie," Faith coached while Jacobi rubbed my back. My contractions were coming closer together, and I knew deep down that it would be time to push soon, but I was anxious.

"Where's Keyon?" I shocked myself, asking a random question between utilizing my breathing exercises as Skyler watched the monitors while Ny adjusted my medication.

"Keyon? Who's Keyon?" Jacobi asked no one in particular.

"Uhm—" Ny spoke as she looked around and ducked out the room quickly.

"AHHHH!" I screamed as another contraction hit me from the side. "Nyoka! Where are you!"

"She left, honey," Skyler spoke warmly as he took over on back duty. "Now, who is this Keyon person exactly?"

Just as I opened my mouth, I was hit again with another contraction; this one hurt more than the first. "SKYLER, I'M READY TO PUUUUUUSH!"

"Oh shit!" Skylar yelped, springing into action. "Nurse, get the team in here!" Out of nowhere, I saw activity swirling around me as my 'baby squad' prepped for the arrival of my son. Faith and Jacobi hugged in the corner, excited to be a part of the action that would finally give them the one thing that would complete their union. I just wanted to push and get back to me.

My son made his entrance into the world loud and in charge. Weighing in at a solid nine pounds even, we knew he had a healthy set of lungs, and after his initial checkup, the doctor determined he was an even healthier baby boy. Faith and Jacobi were nice enough to let me hold him, leaving the room while we had a moment.

I counted his fingers and toes, sniffing his hair as I held him tightly. "Mommy loves you, baby," I whispered as he smiled sweetly in his sleep. Rubbing my face against his silky hair, I wanted his features to stay in my memory forever. Everyone I knew told me that babies fresh out the womb didn't have a look, but my son looked like me and Keyon, and that hurt like hell. In a perfect world, Keyon would be by my side; gushing like a proud father and taking pictures to send to his family and friends. But we didn't live in a perfect world; shit happened, and we had to make those decisions that we hoped were right, being the ones that paid the ultimate price if they weren't.

The door opened and Katie, my caseworker from the adoption agency, peeked her head in. "Leonie? I'm so sorry to interrupt, but—"

"I know, I know. It's time, right?" I wiped the wetness from my face and sniffed as I kissed my baby boy one more time.

"Uhm, we have a slight problem."

"Problem? What kind of problem?"

"There's someone here who says he didn't consent for his son to be adopted. Leonie, I thought you told us—"

"What? Katie, what are you talking about?"

The door opened and Keyon stepped in with Nyoka creeping in sheepishly behind him. "Leonie, I couldn't let you do it. I'm sorry, but you two need to talk," my best friend spoke hurriedly, grabbing Katie by the arm and pulling her out of the room as she walked out. "Come on, girl. You might have to find them people another baby, and I know just where you can look," I heard her voice as the door shut.

I opened my mouth to speak, but quickly clamped it shut as Keyon reached over and gently removed my baby from my arms. With one hand gripping the back of his head and the other underneath his bottom, Keyon stared down at him with the look of a proud father overjoyed at the birth of his first child. Running his finger across his cheek, I saw the blanket move as our son wiggled himself comfortable in his father's palm.

"Why didn't you just tell me you were in labor? I would've been here for you," he gently scolded me as our baby frowned in agreement with his father.

"I didn't want to complicate things with you and your wife."

"Fuck Jenessé, this is my son. I'm always gonna be here for him, no matter what she says."

"Keyon, I've already signed the paperwork for him to be adopted," I spoke quietly. "The couple is here from California and ready to take him home. It's an open adoption, so we can see him whenever we want. I was just saying goodbye—"

"Leonie, I don't care what you say, I'm not consenting to you giving away my first son. You just gonna have to come up with a plan B."

∞

Sitting on the expansive front porch of the plantation style home on the ocean's edge on Hilton Head Island, I marveled at the peace and serenity of my current situation. The moss on the weeping willow trees whispered to me the tales of the island's previous occupants that were now long gone as I sat lost in thought.

Keyon refused to allow his son (who he named Keyon Jr. before we left the hospital), to be adopted by Faith and Jacobi, or anyone else for that matter. He then had the nerve to give me an ultimatum: keep his baby or he would make my life hell. As the newly appointed deputy chief of police in Charleston, I had no doubt that he didn't get there strictly from his father-in-law's doing, so I agreed for the time being. Now, I thought that we would be going back to my townhouse to figure some things out, but for the SECOND time in my life, I was wrong again.

My son's father had me ESCORTED, sirens and all, ninety miles away from my home to a house he owned in Hilton Head, passed down to him when his father passed away. The officers made sure the house was safe and secure before they left me in the most beautiful spot in South Carolina ALONE. I wasn't mad, per sé, I just wished I had some company of the male persuasion to keep my time occupied.

Katie called my phone back to back for two weeks before she got the hint that I wasn't giving Keyon Jr. up for nothing in the world. Oh, but she definitely tried it, though: leaving voicemails on my phone threatening to call the police and file a report for the kidnapping of a baby that she would've obtained illegally anyway. I couldn't consent for anyone to adopt KJ now that his father resurfaced from out of the blue; however, she seemed to feel that a little coercing on her part would get KJ in her claws. After a conversation with Ny, I found out that Katie was in the baby selling business, and KJ would've been a quick $25k from Faith and Jacobi. Since she was all about the Benjamins, she'd already been paid half of her retainer and would receive the other half once I signed the paperwork. The newly promoted deputy chief got a nice raise and commendation from that bust.

I didn't want to ask the obvious, but it was a question in my mind: how was Keyon going to tell his wife about our son? The same son that he created on the trip where she decided that 'she needed more time'? Personally, I wanted to tell her myself and wipe that smirk right off her face, but I decided to let him handle it.

Contrary to what I thought during my entire pregnancy, I loved being a mother. Keyon encouraged me to breastfeed, and I enjoyed spending that time bonding with my baby. We often sat on the porch and watched the breeze blow the trees back and forth as the sounds of the Atlantic Ocean beating gently against the shore lulled my baby to sleep. There was a small garden in the back that was covered in overgrown weeds, and I cleaned everything up before planting some turnip greens, tomatoes, and peppers in addition to the honeysuckle that grew wild on the island. Keyon visited us every weekend, and I loved cooking for my man while he spent time with our baby; it was almost as if we were a happy family. Almost.

KJ was about a month and a half when I decided it was time for me and Keyon to have a conversation. I had to get back to work, and I hoped he didn't think I was going to sit cooped up in a house on Hilton Head to be his kept woman. Hell, it was 2017; this ain't the old south. Women don't just sit back and keep their mouths shut while their men had their cake and ate it too; we spoke up for ourselves and our babies. Keyon was a police officer; anything could happen and his wife would be his sole heir while my baby didn't get shit. I wasn't playing those games, and he needed to know that now rather than later.

Hearing his car pull into the driveway, I thought nothing of it; after putting KJ down for his nap a while ago, I started to prepare his father's dinner. The front door opened and closed, and I heard what sounded like two sets of footsteps walk through the living room toward the kitchen. "I didn't know if you wanted chicken or steak tonight, so I decided to smother you a T-Bone and put the chicken in the refrigerator if you decided—" I stopped when I turned around, and my heart felt like it dropped down to the soles of my feet.

"I don't eat steak, but I'll have some chicken, if you don't mind," Jenessé's shrill tone grated my ears as she stood in the doorway to the kitchen with her arms crossed over her chest and hip poked out.

"Actually, I do mind. I just ran out of rat poisoning, but you're not allergic to arsenic, are you? Do you prefer baked or grilled?" I smiled brightly, clutching a butcher knife in my hand.

Keyon looked back and forth between us with a smile on his face, but I didn't see shit funny. I would snap her skinny ass neck with my bare hands and bury this bitch underneath this house before I allowed her to come in here and take away my happiness. Yea, he might've been a police officer and all, but considering the circumstances, I'm sure he would understand.

"Tuh." She sucked her teeth and rolled her eyes at me again, just like she did on the boat. "Only reason I'm here is because Keyon said he had something important to show me. I guess it's 'bout that time for you to be packing your shit, hun, 'cause I'm loving this house." She waved her hand to dismiss me as she walked back into the living room, glancing at the ceilings.

"Keyon, after you get your little tenant out of here, we gonna have to get some contractors in here to give me an open floor plan. I don't like how closed off this kitchen is. And this tiny space won't fit my island that I need right here." She stood halfway in the living room and waved her arms in a circle.

"He got something important to show you?" I giggled. "Girl, I got something to TELL you. While you in here redecorating like this is an episode of 'House Hunters

Renovation', your husband got a son upstairs asleep. Keep your voice down, bitch."

"A son?" she busted out laughing. "With you? Why would he settle for yo' fat ass when he got me?"

"While you was on the boat getting your beauty rest, boom, your fiancé was licking me from my rolls to my toes in Jamaica, hunny," I laughed with her. "It's ok, I know you pissed, but hold ya bladder in my house. This milkshake brought your man to the yard, damn right, it's better than yours," I sang, turning around and dropping it low; sweeping my hair up in the back, I twerked for her husband as she stood with her mouth dropped open in shock.

"Keyon!" she screamed, turning to him as he cheered me on. "KEYON! IS THIS TRUE?"

"Aye, aye, aye... damn girl...." Keyon mumbled as he watched me for a few seconds longer. "Jenessé, it's very true. I love this woman," he spoke, finally able to stop instigating the fight brewing between us.

"You... how? How can you love someone that looks like that?" she frowned her face in disgust, pointing at me. Wrapping my robe tighter around me, I stood up and matched her look.

"If you mean someone who is smart, funny, caring, empathetic, sweet, loving, and thoughtful... it's easy," he smiled, wrapping his arms around me as he kissed my neck. "I knew from the first time I met her that she was my queen."

"Your... your qu— YOUR QUEEN!" Jenessé roared. "KEYON!"

"Jenessé, listen,"

"No, YOU listen! In all the time we've known each other, you've NEVER said anything on that level to me! Why would you marry me knowing your heart belonged to someone else?"

"Are we really gonna do this here?" he questioned, closing his eyes to rub his temples as he took a deep breath in and blew it out.

"Yes, we're really gonna do this here!" she replied, nodding her head vigorously in his direction.

"I don't want to be a part of this," I spoke, turning to head upstairs with junior. Maybe I was being a little petty earlier, but these were married folks. Why else would Keyon bring her here knowing I was here if it wasn't to tell her about Keyon Jr.?

"No, baby, you can stay," he insisted, stopping me before I walked out. "She's the one that'll be leaving."

"Keyon!" we both yelled at the same time. "That's your wife!" I pointed in her general direction.

"I'm your wife! She can go!"

"Jenessé, I brought you here to not only tell you about my son, but also to tell you we're not married."

"WHAT! KEYON WHAT DO YOU MEAN WE AREN'T MARRIED!"

"Jenessé, stop being so overdramatic; you know your father begged me to marry you," he asserted. "Remember when you and your mother started planning the wedding? How you were so insistent on everything being just right, so you chose to not include me in anything that had to do with it?"

"Baby, I didn't want you to get cold feet," she whined with her arms outstretched. I saw her take three steps in his direction as he turned toward me.

"Guess who our officiant was?"

"Who?"

"Pierre St. Claude."

I ran his name briefly through my memory; it was on the tip of my tongue who he was related to. "Wait, wait, wait. Ny's cousin, Pierre?"

Keyon nodded his head with the cutest smile before bending down to kiss my lips. "Yup."

"WHO IS NY!" Jenessé screamed, stomping her foot so hard I knew we'd be repairing a hole in the hardwood soon.

"My best friend," I snickered, wrapping my arms around him. "What Pierre do, baby?"

"Signed the marriage certificate in the wrong spot," he expressed as I caressed his face.

"Wait, Keyon! KEYON! That's an easy fix, baby! We can just go down to the courthouse and—"

"Nah, I'm good," he interrupted her in mid-sentence. "I just told you this woman is my queen, and I don't want to sacrifice what we building to be with you."

"KEYON! WHAT ABOUT US!"

"What about us?"

"I love you, baby..." she begged, revenge tears rolling down her face. "Keyon, I forgive you. We can get past this, please! KEYON, PLEASE!"

"I'm not asking for you to forgive me, not asking you anything other than to leave our home," he spoke, walking her to the door.

"I'm not leaving this house," she stopped in the doorway, folding her arms across her chest and digging her heels in the jamb. "I don't care what no piece of paper say; we ARE married and this is MY house!"

"Jenessé—"

"Nah, baby girl, you not leaving Keyon's house. You're leaving MY house," I gently nudged my son's father out the way. "You don't want these problems, hunny, trust me." Reaching around her to unlock the storm door, I forcefully pushed her onto the front porch and pulled the door shut behind her, sliding the lock to the right. "And, don't forget MY husband is a police officer, fuck with that cruiser if you want to!" I yelled out before shutting the oak door amid her screams.

"How do you expect her to get off your porch, Leonie?" Keyon laughed at the scene in front of him.

"You unlock that door and you'll be out there right along with her, Keyon Braithwaite Senior." I took his hand in mine and led him upstairs. "She can call an Uber."

"Yes, ma'am." He bit me on my left thigh as he climbed the steps behind me. "And what you 'bout to do?"

"Guess how old Junior is today, love?"

"Six weeks, ain't he?"

"Yup. Guess what else?" I teased, stopping on the last step to face him as he kissed a line from my belly button to my face.

"What else, beautiful?" he growled, wrapping an arm around my waist and licking my face.

"Keyon?"

"Mhmm—"

"You don't even know what I was about to say," I moaned as he picked me up and carried me to our bedroom.

"I know what you was about to say." He laid me down gently and laid on top of me, grinding his sex against mine as he leaned in to bite my neck.

"What you think I was about to say?"

Grazing his hand down my arm, he raised up slightly as he tucked my hand in his pants. "You can touch it baby," he whispered too late; I already had both hands wrapped around that pretty love stick of his that I wanted to put in my mouth since that night in Jamaica.

"Remember when you took my goodies in Jamaica?" I cooed as he peck kissed me all over my body.

"You can't take from the willing," he pulled my silk kimono robe open to reveal my surprise for the evening; a turquoise silk and lace corset with matching boy shorts. "Ooo, look what my baby did for me," his eyes shone brightly as his uttered words saturated my panties.

"Keyon..." My mouth was suddenly moist. I swallowed briefly as his tongue darted out to touch my lips.

"Yes, sweetness?" he skimmed his fingertips from my forehead down across my cheek and ended up on my chin as he raised my head to meet his lips, suctioning my lips as he parted them with his thick tongue.

"How did we get here? Who would've thought I'd be with you?" I met his eyes, and he gave me his undivided attention.

"Leonie, when I laid eyes on you and you told me your story about how that boy stole your car, I could tell there was something there; you were my 'love at first sight' love. I saw a good woman who should be married walking in the spirit of a girlfriend. I knew then that I was the one who would take you out of that mindset and uplift you; it was my job to be both your strength and your weakness."

"But I stopped calling you. Why am I still worth that sacrifice?"

"When a man finds a woman worth sacrificing for, there is no boundary that he won't overcome..." he kissed my nose, "no obstacle that stands in his way..." he kissed my forehead, "no limit to what he'll endure for his woman." He kissed my lips as a tremor shook my body. "Leonie, I just wanna mean the most to you," he whispered the last part, touching his forehead to mine.

"You mean everything to me, Keyon," I spoke, running my fingertips along his spine, opening my legs slightly wider. His words had love running through every fiber of my being. Resting my hand on his chest, I realized my body vibrated in sync with his heartbeat. Sliding himself closer to my love cave, I felt his dick pulsate against the French lace covering me from being completely naked; my skin tingled at his touch.

"Can I touch you here?" he questioned, grazing his fingers across my chest. "Touch your deepest feelings, right here in your heart, baby?" He slid my panties to the side. "Make love to you the right way… forever," he whispered, gradually slipping inside of my drenching wet folds; I heard the material that used to be my panties rip away from my flesh as he eliminated the barrier keeping him from my stickiness.

"Right there, Keyon," I whimpered as he pulled my arms up above my head and held them together with one hand as the other raised my thigh to rest my leg on his shoulder. I turned slightly to my side as he bit my neck and shoved himself deeper and deeper inside. "Fuck me, baby."

Lowering my leg, he slid from between my thighs and flipped me over roughly, pulling me up by my waist until I was on all fours on the bed. "You want me to fuck you, girl?" he growled in my ear, spreading my cheeks and slamming inside of me forcefully. Grabbing a handful of my hair, he reached around and fingered my pussy as he rammed himself deeper and deeper. "You want me to fuck you like that?"

The pain from him pulling my hair hurt like hell, but when he bit me on the same side of my neck as I bit him on that hot, steamy night in Jamaica… I ain't gonna lie, that move alone had me creaming on his dick within a matter of seconds. "YES, KEYON!"

"Say it again, dammit." He pinched my nipple with one hand while rubbing my nub harder and harder as I heard our skin smacking together, feeling our juices running down my inner thighs. "I ain't tell you that you can come yet, did I?"

"FUCK! KEYON, FUCK!" I turned around to see him sweating hard with a concentrated look on his face. Seeing me staring at him, he dug his fingers in my skin before leaning in and pecking me on the lips, giving me EVERY. LAST. INCH.

Out of nowhere, he pulled out of me and ended up underneath me; I felt his teeth on my nipples as he grabbed my hips and sat me down on his thick pole. "You a bad girl tonight, ain't you? Mmhmm… I'ma teach you to come when I tell you to tonight." Looking down, I caught a glimpse of his teasing smile as he uttered underneath me.

"I'ma show your ass why you need to ask me before you give me that good stuff, you hear me, Leonie?" Keyon was showing out, and I loved it. As he clenched my hips tighter and wrapped his legs around mine, junior started crying.

We both sighed and smiled at each other in love as sweat poured off our bodies; I realized my hair was plastered to my face as my future husband framed my face with his hands and stared deeply in my eyes. "You lucky my son woke up, I was about to split your ass in two and fuck the life out of both of y'all," he snickered.

"Well, let me go put him back to sleep so I can see what you working with," I grinned, too sore to move.

"Mmhmm." He rolled from underneath me and smacked me on my ass. "Yo' sexy ass ain't going nowhere. Daddy will get the baby, then he'll be back to take care of you, ok?" he mumbled, kissing my lips.

"You'll bring me some ice, Daddy?"

"Want some water with it?" He paused at the bedroom door, waiting for my response.

"Just ice. I need something to put between my—"

"I'll come back and take care of that, you don't need no ice," he smirked sexily, licking his lips before flicking his tongue in my direction.

Chapter 9

Present day

Me and KJ were out for the day at the Children's Museum; he loved seeing the colors throughout the building. Keyon read a bunch of books for first time parents and insisted that we expose him to colors early rather than later, because he was raising the next Picasso. Since I had to take his books back to the library, I went in to look around for another book by Fatima; Ny had me officially hooked. I subscribed to her mailing list and got an email about one of her latest books that reminded me of my life with Tristan. It was about a woman who was being physically and emotionally abused that got pregnant by an asshole, then met the sweetest man who would go to the end of the world for her. The asshole had this poor woman convinced that they should be together and she wasn't deserving of anything outside the piece of love he gave her and the rest of Detroit. On the other hand, Prince Charming and his connections had something for that ass when he tried to take that baby.

Heading back to the urban fiction section, I grabbed the last copy of *Shoulda Let You Go* and Keyon's books that he had on hold. Losing track of time at the library running off at the mouth with Dorinda, I looked out the library windows and saw the sun preparing to set behind the building. "Oh my goodness! I gotta get home and get started on Keyon's dinner, he's gonna kill me!"

"And it's Valentine's Day too? I hope you got something nice planned, since you in the library instead of spending the day with that handsome husband of yours."

"It is?" I looked around the library and realized everything was decorated in pink pastels and red satiny hearts; Cupid was poised at the front door to shoot his arrows of love all over Charleston. "You think you can get Tamala Mann to sing at my funeral? If not her, I'll settle for Kirk Franklin. You know he gon' preach first!"

"I highly doubt your husband is gonna kill you," Dorinda laughed. "I've never known the chief of police to be violent toward anybody, and the whole town knows he's in love with you!"

"Damn, it feels good to be in love!" I yelled out, doing a little praise dance. Half of the library turned around to frown up in my direction, but I didn't care. I'd shout it from the top of the building if I wasn't afraid of heights.

"Get your butt out of here, Leonie, before you get me fired," she chastised playfully.

"I'll see you next week, girl!" I waved, pushing KJ's stroller out of the building. Balancing the stroller's handle while trying to hold the door open, I was thankful when someone behind me held the door open long enough for me to push the baby through. "Thank you," I turned my head slightly and acknowledged their assistance.

"No problem, Leonie. How are you doing? I see you looking good."

Turning around completely, I looked in Tristan's eyes with disdain. "You cannot be serious right now!" I screamed. "When did you get out?"

He stepped in to give me a hug, and I backed away from his touch. "I can't even get a hug?"

"Tristan, you— AAAAARGH! NO!"

"Leonie, look, I know I took you through a lot. Spending those couple of years behind bars helped me to see what I did to you," he spoke truthfully. "I'm a changed man, Leonie. I meditate now, I go to church. I pray with my wife—"

"Your common-law wife?"

"My life partner; me and Nyana were married when I got out."

"Is that the woman you were with for—"

"No."

"No?" I was suddenly curious about what was going on in his life since the incident. "What happened?"

Taking a deep breath in, he pinched the bridge of his nose before blowing it out. "You talking about Ameri?"

"I guess so, I don't know these women." I motioned for him to follow me to a bench where we could sit and talk for a few minutes without people all in our conversation.

"You ever been with somebody for years and realize that they weren't what you were looking for?"

"How so?"

"She was too perfect. Did everything I asked, never argued, always forgave me. Even after she found out about me and you when that police officer dropped my stuff off at the house, she still forgave me and said we could work it out. I didn't want a doormat, I wanted a woman. Had to leave her alone," he grumbled. Suddenly, I realized the real reason Tristan treated me like he did. Thinking back, I could pinpoint the moments when his love would turn to verbal abuse. *I never said no.*

"Isn't that what men want? The perfect woman who doesn't complain?"

"That's not what I wanted. I thought I did when I was out here in the world, but when I got locked up, I had time to think."

"And what did you come up with?"

"First and foremost, I want you to know that everything I did to you wasn't your fault. That was me not dealing with my own insecurities and projecting them on you. You know, Leonie, you might not ever forgive me for the way I treated you, and I understand if you don't. But, if one day you find it in your heart, I would appreciate it," he spoke from the heart.

"I forgive you, Tristan."

"It's James."

"That's right, it is. I was just so used to calling you Tristan that—"

"I know, I know." Dropping his head, he fidgeted with his hands before he spoke again. "Leonie when I first approached you, I was attracted to you, for real. I know what the officer said, and what those other women said, but you are a beautiful woman. That night when I took you to meet my aunt, she told me I'd be a damn fool to stay in a relationship with you because I was gonna go bankrupt trying to feed you."

"I knew I should've let her ass have it that night," I fumed. *Ol' decrepit bitch.*

"She kept going and going; every time I talked to her, she had something else to say about your weight. I got tired of defending you, so I stopped."

"Damn, James, for real?" I frowned. "I would've defended my relationship with you to the world."

"That's the thing, Leonie. I know you would've. For me, though, I saw it as she was finally talking about something other than me living off my 'common-law wife'," he air quoted.

"You know, some relationships are optional, not mandatory. Sometimes, it could be sacrificing that relationship from a toxic person that has their own issues in order to preserve your sanity," I advised. "I know that's your aunt, but what's more important to you: her opinion or your peace of mind?"

"I'm finding that out now," he nodded in agreement.

"So, tell me about your wife. I'm guessing she's the opposite of Ameri?"

"The exact opposite," he echoed. "She has her own opinion and doesn't mind expressing it. We argue, we disagree; yet she still loves me and I love the hell out of her." I saw a gleam in his eye that I'd never seen before as he spoke about his wife. "The passion is there; I realize she is what I've been looking for all these years. When I heard you scream out in there, I wanted to stand on the table and yell the same thing because— damn!"

Had James and I had this conversation a while ago, it would've gone a lot differently. I'm sure he would be good and slapped by now. Being in love with someone who loved me— AAAAHHHH being in love with someone who loved ME! I could have this conversation with James and call him by his name without having any other thoughts other than to go home, cook for my family, and lay up under my man. My phone went off in my purse and I knew who it was. Answering it without looking at the screen, I smiled as I caught a glance at his profile picture. "I'm on my way, love."

"Just checking, babe. I was worried about you and junior," Keyon's voice was the harmony in my soul; I fell in love all over again each time he spoke. "I cooked spaghetti and meatballs, and the garlic bread is warming in the oven. Hurry up before it burns."

"On my way love; I bumped into James at the library and he was telling me about what's been going on with him."

"James Montgomery?"

"Mmhmm."

"Tell him I said thanks. Come home, baby."

"Give me five minutes." I cheesed before hanging up. This man worked a full shift as the chief of police since old man Watson stepped down last year, yet he still found time to cook for ME.

"I'm glad to see that you found someone that puts the smile on your face that I should have." James smiled with me. "Again, I apologize for any time that I made you feel less than a woman, and me and my wife will pray for the success of you and your family."

"Thank you. Keyon and I will pray for your family as well. Good luck to you, James." I gave him a sisterly hug before loading Junior into the truck to head home.

Riding to our home across the water in Mount Pleasant, I could've sworn I was being followed. Shaking it off as nothing, I got to the house and Keyon met me in the driveway. "Hey, babe," he pecked me on the cheek, reaching in the back seat to grab the stroller as I grabbed junior. "Did you get some more baby books from the library?"

"Yea, and Dorinda told me to create an account for junior on Khan Academy if we decide to do the homeschool thing," I spoke, walking in the house. Kicking off my heels before placing junior in his playpen, I walked into the kitchen to wash my hands when I heard a commotion on the porch.

"Keyon, will you look at the pictures, dammit!" I heard a woman's voice hissing lowly so I wouldn't hear her. "I'm telling you, that fat bitch ain't no better than me!"

"Jenessé, what do you not understand when I say I don't want you? Do you not understand basic English? Let me say it in Spanish: *No te quiero.* You want it in Italian? *Non ti voglio.* French? *Je ne veux pas de toi.* German? *Ich will dich nicht.* Wait, you Creole right? *Mwen pat vle ou.* Are we done here?"

Look at my baby, all bilingual and stuff, I thought as I ear hustled behind the door. I wasn't gonna say nothing to her; Keyon would take care of all that.

"Keyon, please! I'm trying to tell you about that fa—"

"My wife ain't gonna be too many more fat bitches, you really need to understand and comprehend that," he began. "I don't hit women, but you trying my patience right now." I heard his voice change, he hadn't had that tone in his voice since the last time we saw his... ex-wife? *Wait, ex-fiancée. They weren't married,* I snickered to myself.

"Oh, I'm trying your patience, but your 'wife' out here hugged up on her ex like they trying to get back together in front of your son." She sucked her teeth and probably cut her tongue in the process.

"Jenessé, you've known me for a while now. Obviously, not as well as I would assume you would, being that we were something like married, but we've shared space. What do you think I'm gonna say?"

"What do you mean?"

"Just that. You claim you love me, you want us to work. Pop quiz: we're married, hypothetically speaking. One of my exes... let's say Marion, shows up on our doorstep with pictures of you hugged up with one of your exes. What do you think my next move is?"

"Keyon... uhmm... shit, this ain't school! What you mean, 'pop quiz'?" she screamed.

"Keep your voice down, my son isn't exposed to negativity in his space. We raising a gentleman. Answer my question, though."

"Well... uhmm... you'd come in the house demanding to know who I was hugged up with, and why," she stammered.

"If I just told you we raising a gentleman, what makes you think I'd be yelling over an assumption? You just proved my point," he spoke calmly.

"But Keyon—"

"Have a nice life, Jenessé. Tell your father I said hello." Sticking his hands in the pockets of his slacks, he stared her in the eyes firmly as she turned and sheepishly slouched down the steps. "How did I handle it, babe?" he called out to me inside the house.

"Huh? Oh, I was just looking for something—"

"Behind the door?" he chuckled, waving at Jenessé one more time as her tires screeched on the pavement. "You didn't have anything to worry about, love. I trust you."

"I know, but—"

"No buts. You my baby carrying my baby." Joining him on the porch to show Jenessé as she looked back at us one more time what marriage excellence was, he reached over and rubbed my baby bump. "We ain't got matching fang tats for nothing."

"Keyon, you so petty," I giggled, the bite mark on my neck tingling.

"I'm petty, but you pregnant. Ain't it Valentine's Day? Come on so I can feed you and rub your feet."

Standing behind me as he held the screen door open, we walked back in the house together with his hand on my butt.

"You keep acting like this, I might think you like me," I giggled, grabbing junior from his playpen before heading to the kitchen.

"I might like you a little."

"That's all I ask, Keyon. That's all I ask." I smiled.

∞

"Baby, did I tell you KJ said his first word today!" I cheered as he walked into the bedroom from the bathroom wearing nothing but a pair of boxers. Climbing onto the bed next to me, he pecked me on my lips, sliding his hand slowly down my leg and squeezing my thigh. I saw the worries of the world etched across his face melt away as he focused on my words.

"Oh, yea? What did he say?"

"Daddy, of course." I smiled as I leaned in to outdo his kiss, our tongues dancing together sensually as he caressed my baby bump.

"I'm proud of him, but I'm especially proud of you. You're a great woman and an even better mother."

I pushed a lock of hair behind my ear, lowering my head with a tiny smile. Keyon had me blushing whenever he complimented me for something small; I loved him and my little family. "I just want to mean the most to you, babe," I spoke.

"Don't be using my words trying to get me to like you," he grinned.

"Oh, so now you like me."

"Come here, baby," Keyon Sr. curled his finger in my direction. Scooting over to sit on his lap, I rested my head on his shoulder as he stroked my hair. "Are you gonna be in love with me? I want you and need you to beeeee, yeah," he sang my favorite song by Luther Vandross in my ear.

"I will always be in love with you, baby." Turning to look him in the eye, he bent down and peck kissed the tip of my nose. "Keyon?"

"Yes, love?"

"Happy Valentine's Day, baby. I love you, Mr. Braithwaite."

"Every day I have you is Valentine's Day," he whispered to my soul. "I love you too, Mrs. Braithwaite."

The End

Thanks for reading! If Keyon and Leonie's story made you wanna grab your boo and slow dance to Luther Vandross by candlelight, please drop me a review! And if my books are 'new to you', I'd love it if you signed up for my mailing list to learn more about my work! Go to www.fatimasbooks.com and get a coupon code for 10% off your first purchase on my website!

Did you get my last couple of books? Click here:

Shoulda Let You Go: http://amzn.to/2j72Eny

If Loving You Is All I Gotta Do: A New Year Love Story: http://bit.ly/IfLovingYou2

Check out my full catalog on my website: www.fatimasbooks.com!

Follow me on social media!

Facebook: http://facebook.com/authorfatimamunroe

Fatima's Book Group

Twitter: http://twitter.com/fatima_munroe

IG: http://instagram.com/fatimamunroe

CPSIA information can be obtained
at www.ICGtesting.com
Printed in the USA
LVHW022056290120
645191LV00017B/1294

9 781986 596299